The Italian Cure

The Italian Cure

Melodie Campbell

ORCA BOOK PUBLISHERS

Library and Archives Canada Cataloguing in Publication

Title: The Italian cure / Melodie Campbell.
Names: Campbell, Melodie, 1955– author.
Series: Rapid reads.
Description: Series statement: Rapid reads

Identifiers: Canadiana (print) 20190168994 | Canadiana (ebook) 20190169001 |
ISBN 9781459821125 (softcover) | ISBN 9781459821132 (PDF) |
ISBN 9781459821149 (EPUB)

Classification: LCC PS8605.A54745 I83 2020 | DDC C813/.6—dc23

Library of Congress Control Number: 2019943973
Simultaneously published in Canada and the United States in 2020

Summary: A woman travels to Italy to cure her broken heart in this short novel.

*Orca Book Publishers is committed to reducing the consumption
of nonrenewable resources in the making of our books. We make
every effort to use materials that support a sustainable future.*

Orca Book Publishers gratefully acknowledges the support for its publishing
programs provided by the following agencies: the Government of Canada,
the Canada Council for the Arts and the Province of British Columbia
through the BC Arts Council and the Book Publishing Tax Credit.

Design by Ella Collier
Cover illustration by gettyimages.ca/Cenari

ORCA BOOK PUBLISHERS
orcabook.com

Printed and bound in Canada.

23 22 21 20 • 4 3 2 1

For Dave. One last dance.

One

"Italy!" Aunt Della yelled over the phone. "Do you have a passport?"

"Yes," I said. We live in Buffalo. You need a passport to go over the border to shop in Toronto, which is the biggest city around. But what was this about Italy?

"Rome, Sorrento and the Amalfi Coast. Pompeii! Remember that contest I entered last month?" she said.

I leaned back against the deli counter where I worked. "Not exactly," I said, smiling. Typical Aunt Del. She always assumed you knew everything she did.

My aunt is a widow. She likes to talk on the phone. Okay, she likes to talk, period. And then she said the words that changed my life.

"I won! Seven days in Italy for two. And Charlie, you're coming with me!"

I sucked in air. "Italy? Are you kidding me?" The land of sunshine, great food and romance? I'd always dreamed of going there.

"Pack your bags. We're going in two weeks. I'll clear it with your uncle Vince." She hung up.

I stared at the phone in my hand. Maybe if I stared at it long enough, other good things would happen.

My older cousin Rickie poked his dark curly head out from the back room. "Who was that on the phone?"

"Aunt Della," I said, looking up. "She just won a one-week trip to Italy, and she's taking me!"

Rickie laughed. "You and Aunt Del, together for one week solid. Are you sure about that?"

I stared at him.

"Remember last year at my wedding when she did cartwheels across the dance floor?" he said. "And when she challenged the ushers to a chugging contest? And won?"

"She's a character." I smiled, thinking of that reception. I remembered what she had told me afterward: *Why be boring?*

But Rickie had a point. Was this crazy? We'd never been away together before. Sure, I had spent time with her and Uncle Joe at their house. They didn't have any kids of their own. She used to take me for overnights when I was young to give my parents a break. I'd always felt special and much loved in those times.

"Earth to Charlie," he said. "You okay if I open up now? It's nearly time, and people are outside waiting."

"Okay," I said. "But can you hand me that roll of cash-register tape up there first? I'll need it pretty soon." I pointed to the shelf above the back counter.

Rickie reached up with one hand easily. "Sucks to be short," he said.

"Great things come in small packages," I shot back.

He grinned as he handed me the roll.

It was true. I'd give a million bucks to be four inches taller. Not that I have a million. And that would just make me average height.

I thanked him for the tape and slipped back to the cash register. Rickie unlocked the glass door. Then he joined me behind the counter to serve customers.

My name is Charlotte, but everyone calls me Charlie. I work in my uncle Vince's deli as a cashier. So getting time off work wouldn't be a problem. Aunt Del would simply tell her younger brother that I was going to Italy with her. I grinned at that. Aunt Del is bossy. She is also colorful and kooky. I love her dearly. Heck, I once wanted to *be* her when I got older.

However, living with her in a hotel room for a week was something I had never done. Should I be worried?

I smiled at the customers traipsing in. What the poop. A free trip to Italy? I was going!

Two

The night before our flight, I got out my apple-green suitcase. It was an old thing, handed down from my aunt when she got a new set. It was soft-sided and a little battered. But it would do. It had wheels, at least, and a pull strap on one end.

I set about finding things to fill it with. And as I did, my mind wandered.

I didn't like to admit it, but Italy had been my dream honeymoon spot. For years I had collected posters and travel brochures of Rome. They were still in the bottom drawer of my dresser, waiting for the day.

I never got the honeymoon. Rob left me after seven years of dating. We even lived together for the last two. My parents weren't keen on that. But Rob thought we should try living together before we got married. He even used the word *married*.

Three months ago, things changed. *He* changed. It wasn't fun anymore, he said. At first I was shocked. I didn't understand. Then I came to realize he was having fun with someone new.

He moved out. At first I wanted to die. Now I had progressed to the stage where I wanted *him* to die. The low-life cheating bastard!

Not only did he rip out my heart. There was also the apartment. He left me with rent I could barely afford to pay. It certainly didn't allow me to save up for trips.

I continued to pack, all the while thinking about the future. My parents had suggested that I move back home temporarily. They were great parents, and I loved them. I could save money if I didn't have this blasted rent to pay. But moving back to my childhood home would be like admitting defeat.

I didn't want them to see how devastated I was over Rob. For lunch and dinner visits, I could cover it up. But if I lived with them...

Also, I knew they were using my old room for Carrie's special equipment. Carrie is my sister, seven years younger than me. Something happened when she was born. She uses a wheelchair and goes to a special school. She's sweet and loyal and very pretty. I couldn't have a nicer sister. The last thing I wanted to do was inconvenience everyone by moving back home.

Carrie and I talked to each other by email every night. It was our way of closing out the day. She told me her struggles, and I shared my woes with her. Emailing each night made us feel closer than when we had actually lived in the same house. I didn't want that to change, and I knew she felt the same way.

My cell phone rang. I knew from the ringtone that it was Aunt Del.

"Here's what I'm taking," she said. "Three pairs of pants, two jackets—one for good, one to wear on the plane over a sweater. We need to layer, because it will be cold here when we leave and warm when we land in Rome. Let's see what else. Several tops and two dresses that pack well. Walking shoes, good shoes and sandals. And don't forget a hat!"

"I won't," I said. Two dresses that packed well? I didn't wear dresses to work. The only dresses I had were for family occasions like weddings and funerals. I'd pack a few summer skirts instead.

"It will be fun sharing this with you," I said. I was missing having someone to share things with. That was the worst part. You came home at the end of the day with lots to talk about, but there was nobody there to talk to anymore.

But it was more than that. And Aunt Del could always read my mind.

"You're a bit lonely now," she said. "And I don't mean just because the stinking turd left."

I smiled. Aunt Del never held back.

"That's true. We did a lot of things as a couple, with other couples," I said. "They don't invite me on my own."

Aunt Del sighed. "Yes, that's the trouble. A newly single woman isn't always welcome in a group where everyone else is married or part of a couple. People feel uncomfortable. I know all about that. When Joe died, the invitations dried up. I had to make new friends."

That was my problem. I needed to make new friends.

She continued. "What you've been through is worse in some ways. Friends have to choose between one person or the other.

If they want to still hang out with the turd, they feel uncomfortable seeing you too. So they choose."

"Rob was the exciting one," I said, feeling a lump start in my throat. "It's no wonder they chose him. I'm boring."

"You're not boring!" she said. "You're nice and kind and dependable. Look how you are with Carrie. Those qualities are worth more than you can imagine."

To be honest, I wasn't feeling very nice at the moment. Bloodthirsty was the word that came to mind. I kept imagining our old couple friends with a new person in their lives. Rob's new girlfriend.

"Remember," said Aunt Del. "With every end comes a new beginning."

We said good night and hung up. I continued packing.

Aunt Del was a dear. I knew she was trying to make me feel better. And to be truthful, I was over the worst of it. But oh, I missed being in a couple.

That wasn't all. I had no confidence in myself anymore. It had all been such a shock. I didn't see the breakup coming. There must have been signs, but I didn't see them. I'd thought we were good.

Could I ever trust my judgment again?

Someone, somewhere, needed to invent a cure for the broken heart.

Snap out of it, I told myself as I clicked the suitcase shut. In less than twenty-four hours, I would be in Rome. *Rome!* And a new adventure would begin.

Three

DAY ONE

"Lost? My luggage is lost?" I couldn't believe what the elderly airport worker was telling me.

Aunt Della groaned beside me. "We left home twenty hours ago. We had to change planes in New York. We hardly had any sleep on the plane. We've been waiting over an hour at the luggage carousel. And now you're telling us her suitcase didn't make it onto the flight?"

The small man shrugged dramatically as only real Italians can do. "Happen every day," he said with a thick accent. "Luggage go walk-about. Will turn up somewhere."

I wanted to throw things. Except the only thing I had to throw was my carry-on. And I wasn't parting with that.

The first day of my trip and already something had gone wrong.

Before I could think of what to do next, a tall gray-haired man came up to us. "Hello there. I saw you on the plane," he said to Aunt Del. "I think we're on your tour. If you need any help, I speak Italian."

"Della Parker," said my aunt, reaching forward to shake hands.

"Della..." repeated the fellow.

"I was named after Della Street," she said.

He looked confused.

"Like on *Perry Mason*. The TV show."

His face cleared. "That should be easy to remember."

"And this is Charlie," she said, gesturing to me.

"Charlie?" said the fellow, scratching his head.

"Don't be dense, Ed!" The high voice came from a woman behind him. "After *Charlie's Angels,* obviously. They're both named after famous television people."

Except the Charlie on *Charlie's Angels* was a man, I thought to myself.

"Actually, her name is Charlotte. Like Charlotte from *Sex and the City*. Everyone just calls her Charlie," said my aunt.

I suppose I look a bit like that actress. My hair is brown like Charlotte's on *Sex and the City*. But my eyes are gray instead of brown. I used them to check out the woman with yellow-blond hair who was now in front of us.

"Hi! I'm Bunny. This is Ed. We're the Hoppers from New York City."

Bunny Hopper. How could I not smile? I once knew a girl named Crystal Sudds, but this was even better. I wondered if she did the bunny hop.

Aunt Del did not disappoint. "I'll bet you're good at dancing," she said.

"I love to dance!" said Bunny, not getting it at all.

I smiled at Bunny, which was easy to do. She had definitely dressed to be noticed. Most people dress for comfort on a plane. Bunny wasn't having any of that. How to describe her? Her skirt was too short. Her blouse was too low. Her hair was too yellow. Her eyebrows were too arched. And those had to be three-inch heels she was wearing.

Not someone I would normally hang out with. But her smile was wonderful. Bunny clearly meant to have a good time on this trip. And I had to admit her cheeriness was catching.

"Hello, beautiful miss!"

I turned my head at the new voice.

"So. You are the lady who lost her clothes." A gorgeous man winked at me. "I am Rocco, your tour guide. Allora, I hear your suitcase has gone on a trip of its own," he said. "No worry. Will turn up. Rocco will make sure."

I was weirdly tongue-tied. I think I blushed. Our tour guide was too good to be true. Tall, black wavy hair, deep-brown eyes and somewhere under thirty-five. Not only that, but no wedding ring!

And here he was, smiling down on me like I was the only one in the vast arrivals area. It was a madhouse. Well, a girl could dream. People were speaking many different languages. The voice coming over the PA system was garbled. I couldn't even make out if it was Italian.

I didn't resist when Rocco took my arm and guided me toward the revolving glass doors. Aunt Del and the others traipsed behind us.

"Here she is!" Rocco said when we cleared the doors. I could see a crowd of people lined up beside a dark-blue-and-white tour bus. It said *Amore Italia* on the side, with a website and a red heart. Easy to remember, I thought.

We joined the line and eventually made it on board. The young bus driver smiled at me when I went past him.

On this trip to the hotel, we were allowed to sit anywhere. As the bus moved away from the curb, Rocco picked up a microphone.

"Welcome, welcome! To Rome and to Amore tours. I am Rocco. Our driver is Tony. And good news, ladies. He is single!" He waited until the giggles died down. "We take you to your hotel now. Your tour starts tomorrow morning after breakfast, which is provided in the hotel. For the rest of the day, you may sleep or walk the streets."

I heard my aunt snort. "My street-walking days are over," she called out.

Gales of laughter erupted from the people around us. Rocco looked blank. I could see the driver got it though.

"One thing to do," he continued. "Put your passports in the safe in your room. We do have pickpockets in Italy, alas." He shrugged in that flamboyant Italian way.

I enjoyed watching him. He was so good-looking. But it was beyond looks and beyond flair. He seemed to be in love with life.

Maybe it would be contagious, I thought. Could Italy cure my broken heart? I hoped so.

Four

"**First things first,**" said Aunt Del as we settled into our hotel room. "It's already afternoon, and we need to do some emergency shopping for you for necessities. What are you missing? Better still, tell me what you brought in your carry-on bag."

I sat down on the narrow bed and opened the small backpack. I recited the contents to my aunt.

"A sweater. An extra pair of socks and underwear. My sandals. A magazine. Two books." Why did I need two books on the plane? If only I'd brought more underwear instead.

I continued. "That package of nuts we bought at the airport. Two granola bars. Earbuds. My phone charger." Thank goodness I'd packed that in my carry-on!

"Hmmm," said my aunt. "So your train case is in the lost suitcase?"

I smiled at the outdated term, *train case*. "Yup. I'll need to get toothpaste and a toothbrush. Maybe a little makeup." I could make do with just lipstick and mascara. I had a hair brush in my purse.

"I have sunscreen you can use. And an extra hat. So maybe it isn't all that bad. I'm glad you put a pair of undies in your carry-on. You can wash one out in the sink each night, and wear the other the next day. Same with socks."

That was a lucky thing. Shopping was something I was trying to avoid. To put it bluntly, I didn't have much money with me. Aunt Del had said to bring two hundred euros.

I could only afford half that. Thing is, I really didn't want her to know how little money I'd brought. A few souvenirs were all I had planned on buying. I was used to being frugal.

Most of our meals were included on the trip. That was a good thing. So my major problem was going to be clothes.

"Let's look at what you're wearing right now," said Aunt Del. "Those black stretchy pants were a good idea to wear on the plane. They'll go with anything."

"They're yoga pants," I said. "They actually fit me." I have trouble getting regular pants to fit. These ones came in petite sizes.

"Good thing you wore running shoes on the plane," she said. "That top is a write-off though."

I looked down at the brown stains on my shirt. The plane had gone through turbulence, and I'd been splashed with lukewarm coffee. The flight attendant had been really apologetic. But it wasn't going to be easy getting large splotches of coffee out of a white shirt.

"No worries," she said. "I have some tops you can borrow."

I felt a chill run down my spine.

My aunt is pretty, with fluffy dark hair and big blue eyes. But she's not exactly my size or age group. She reminds me of Elizabeth Taylor in one of her later plump phases. My aunt loves bright colors. I'm not so flamboyant. We don't have the same taste in clothes.

Aunt Del yawned. "Why don't you check out the little shop in the hotel lobby?" She flopped down on the other bed. "See if you can get most of what you need there. Hopefully, your suitcase will arrive soon. I'm just going to stay here and have a nap, if you don't mind. I'm beat."

I smiled and took a look around our little room. It was much smaller than North American hotel rooms. Two single beds shared a small bedside table between them. The far wall held a lovely arched window looking out upon a courtyard. That was it. The room had no balcony.

I stood, picked up my purse from the bed and walked to the door. To my left was the bathroom. I peeked in. It held the tiniest bathtub I'd ever seen. Everything seemed to be in miniature, including the sink and the gold mirror above it.

And yet the whole suite was charming. Looking back, I could see light streaming in through the lacy sheer draperies. The carved picture frames and headboards were tipped in gold. Everything, down to the cream and peach bed linens, had been chosen with care. It was like a tiny fairy-castle bedroom.

I took a last look around the room. My eyes settled on Aunt Del. Sleeping Beauty waiting for her prince?

She was already in dreamland when I closed the door.

Five

Our room was on the second floor. I didn't bother to use the two-person elevator. The stairwell was at the end of the hall. I dashed down the stairs with new energy.

I was in Rome! Not even lost luggage could dull my excitement.

I paused in the lobby to look around. Our hotel was very nice but not considered first class. I don't know how many stars it had. I figure they didn't have stars way back when it was built.

The stairway had wooden railings that curled up like giant snails at the ends.

The walls were wood-paneled and very decorative. Mirrors reflected the strong sunshine streaming in the front bay windows. I couldn't wait to feel the sun on me. We had just left behind a brutal winter in Buffalo.

I looked for the little gift shop. It was to the left of the main reception counter. The store was deserted except for the elderly clerk behind the counter. The shop had toothpaste, toothbrushes and even socks. I picked up two pairs. A small cosmetics bar carried brand-name products I recognized. I added mascara and one neutral lipstick to my purchases and took everything to the cashier. I gulped when she told me how many euros. But nothing would be wasted, I told myself. All would be useful back home.

I came out of the shop and ran right into Rocco. He put a hand on my arm to steady me.

"Hello, beautiful miss with the gray eyes!"

Rocco's eyes twinkled into mine. "Could you find your needed things in this shop?"

Apparently, I'd forgotten how to talk. I nodded yes. Funny how I felt like a deer in the headlights when Rocco looked at me. I couldn't look away.

I started to tell him what I had been able to get. He laughed and waved his arm impatiently.

"Molto bene! I leave now to do the phoning," he said. "Must go over menus for the tour with our hotels. Each week new people to make problems. So many dietary restrictions." He shook his head.

I understood about that, working in a deli. Gluten-free, lactose-free...customers were always asking for special products.

He strode off, blowing me a kiss. "Ciao-ciao!"

I smiled stupidly after him. I guess ciao-ciao was like our bye-bye.

The tour didn't officially start until the next day. We were on our own for dinner. Aunt Del wanted to try room service and said she would pick up the tab. I was grateful. Money was going to be really tight for me now. So we had a quiet dinner of linguine with mushrooms and chicken, with cannoli for dessert. It was quite yummy.

That night before bed, I emailed Carrie. I told her about the lost luggage.

Aunt Del is lending me some clothes. And a hat that says Princess on it in sequins. Yes, I'm going to be swimming in psychedelic hot pinks, lime greens and purple parrot prints. I hope you're laughing. If fashion police really existed, I'd be taken down by the SWAT team.

That's it for now. We're off to the Colosseum tomorrow.

Love from Rome,
Charlie

Six

DAY TWO

"It's in Australia?" I stared in disbelief at Tony the bus driver.

"Oh dear. This is bad news," said Aunt Del.

I braced myself. That morning I'd had to borrow a top from Aunt Del to wear over my yoga pants. It didn't exactly fit. I was several sizes smaller than her. She was also a few inches taller than me, but that didn't matter so much with tops.

I wasn't kidding when I'd joked to Carrie about the parrot prints. Aunt Del had a thing for parrots. I used one of her colorful scarves to pull the shirt with orange and purple parrots tight around my waist. I would avoid mirrors for the rest of the day.

Tony was sympathetic. "I checked the airline while Rocco was at breakfast. They assure me your suitcase will be here by tomorrow." He had a nice low voice.

"Not to worry, sweetie. You can borrow more of my clothes if you need to." Aunt Del patted my shoulder.

I could see Tony smile as he turned away.

Aunt Del was wearing apple-green pants with a matching knit top that had rabbits on it. The rabbits were eating carrots. It was sort of an Easter/spring theme, this being April. Subdued for her.

A bunch of people were coming out of the lobby. Aunt Del whooped a greeting to Bunny and went off to join them. I didn't follow. There was something I wanted to do first. I turned to Tony.

"Thanks, Tony. I really appreciate you following up with my luggage. I wouldn't know where to start."

He waved an arm in the air. "My pleasure. This happens more often than you'd think. I know the right people to call, and I speak both English and Italian. Hope we can get it to you soon."

I took a closer look at him. He wasn't very tall. Certainly not as tall as Rocco. And where Rocco had movie-star hair, Tony's was medium brown and curly. He also didn't have Rocco's extreme good looks. Tony was average. Not someone you'd notice.

"Tell me something," I said. "You don't seem to have an accent, and Rocco does."

Tony smiled then. "That's because I was born in Chicago. I only came here two years ago." He leaned back against the bus and folded his arms. Strong arms, from hoisting luggage around every day, no doubt.

"But you speak Italian like a native," I said.

"My folks are Italian. We spoke it at home. I have relatives here, and the older ones don't speak much English. Made it easy to get this job. They need people who are bilingual."

I wanted to ask him more, but the others were coming.

Rocco called us over to the bus. "Now gentlemans and beautiful ladies. Today we see the Colosseum and the Forum of ancient Rome. We stop for lunch at local tavolla calda. Rocco takes good care of you, si?"

Tony leaned down to me. "*Tavolla calda* means a diner-type lunch bar. Time to rock and roll." He held out his hand to help me up the steps into the bus.

"We rotate seats each day," said Rocco, behind me. "First seat today, beautiful miss and lady aunt. Then next day people in last seat come to front. Everyone moves back one. That way, fair."

Just watching him gesture made me happy. He was so animated. And it didn't hurt that he called me "beautiful miss." I'd never been called beautiful before. *Cute* was the word I usually got. If I was noticed at all. When you're short, you don't get noticed as much as tall people are.

As people boarded the bus, I took note. Most people on this trip were of retirement age. A few were older. There wasn't really anyone my age, and no one younger. No children.

Of course! This was April. Kids were still in school.

"I think this is a seniors' tour," I whispered to Aunt Del.

"Nonsense!" she said. "Bunny can't be more than fifty. Although she's trying awfully hard to pass for thirty-five. Mutton dressed as lamb."

I hid my smile. "I thought you liked her," I said.

"I do," said Aunt Del, giving me a side glance. "She amuses me. Why be boring?"

And there it was again. The famous line. I made a promise to myself to become less boring.

"Her husband looks older than fifty," I said. I smiled at him as he waited in line to board the bus.

"Ed has to be at least sixty-five," she said, lowering her voice. "This is a second marriage for sure."

Bunny and Ed climbed the stairs, one after the other.

"Della!" yelled Bunny in her girlish voice. "Oh, the seat behind you is taken." She pouted at the couple sitting there.

"Let's sit together at lunch," said my aunt.

"Great!" said Bunny. Her small red mouth beamed a smile. "Ed, don't be a slow poke.

Let's sit in the last seat today, so we can move up to the front seat tomorrow. That way we can all be together for the rest of the trip."

"Wonderful!" said my aunt. "That's smart thinking."

I wasn't sure it was wonderful. But I did like Ed. He lumbered behind Bunny, taking time to smile and tip his sun hat at us. Now there was an old-fashioned gentleman.

The bus was very modern. Someone had said it was a Mercedes. I liked the royal-blue upholstery on the seats. The air conditioning worked well. There was a washroom at the back. That was an important feature, with so many seniors on board.

Rocco had a clipboard and was ticking off names. He started at the back and then came forward. When he got to me, he smiled at my hat. "Ah! So we have a princess on board. Your name is...Charlotte?"

"Charlie," I said, smiling up at him.

"Princess Sharlie," he said. He winked at me. And then he sat down in the row across from us. It was good timing—we were jolted as the bus sped around a corner.

You haven't really seen traffic until you've driven through Rome. Cars and scooters whiz by everywhere. It's crazy. No one seems to stay in a lane. I mentioned this to Aunt Del.

"They just squeeze in where they can and say a prayer," she said. "Stop lights are merely suggestions."

And the horns! All the time, the sound of cars and trucks beeping and honking. I could never drive in this city.

Tony was a pro, of course. He got us to the Colosseum without a single collision.

Rocco got off the bus first. We all piled off after him. He was conversing with a smartly dressed young woman who carried a red umbrella, so we waited. Finally he turned to us.

"Now, peoples!" he said. "Maria will be your guide through the Colosseum and Forum. She carries the red umbrella so you can find her. Stay close to her. You have two hours here. Then meet back here for the Forum, si?"

We dutifully followed Maria. The Colosseum was immense. I marveled that so much of it was still standing after two thousand years. The ancient limestone walls had an almost reddish cast to them when the sun hit in a certain way.

In those two hours Maria told us more about Roman history than I'd ever known. What a fascinating place! Also, what a horrific one. Christians fed to lions...gladiators fighting to the death. I didn't go down into the gladiator tunnels, even though it was included in our tour. Too grim for me. Instead I stayed in the stands and watched a stray cat sleeping on the warm stone. It was one of many.

Ed came up beside me. He gestured to the cat. "That reminds me of a poem I had to memorize in school." He started to recite it.

> Colosseum cat
> Streak of silver in sun
> Walks the ruins with
> Caesar's ghost.

"Nice," said Tony, who had come up behind us. "Except it would be Nero's ghost. The Colosseum wasn't built yet in Caesar's time."

"I didn't know that," said Ed. He sounded impressed.

Tony shrugged. "I'm a history buff. Never can stay away from ruins."

"Do they let you in the gates for free if you work for a tour company?" I asked.

"Oh no." Tony shook his head. "I was lucky this time because one couple didn't show up for the trip. They canceled at the last minute. We buy the site passes well in advance. I've got one for Pompeii too. That's my favorite ancient site."

He looked down at his watch. "I'll catch up with you after the Forum." He saluted to Ed and smiled at me. I watched him stride out of sight.

Seven

Ed and I caught up with Aunt Del and Bunny. The Roman Forum was also worth seeing, although it wasn't quite as impressive as the Colosseum. More of it was in ruins, but that made it almost more romantic, in a way.

Gray, dusty white and soft brown were the dominant colors here. We were told these buildings had once been colorful. But no paint remained on the marble columns and ruined buildings. It made a solemn contrast to the green of the grass and our colorful clothes.

As Maria talked, I could clearly see how people would have lived their lives back then.

They would shop at the market and worship at the temples. In fact, we were told, originally the Forum was a marketplace. Later government buildings were added. The Senate House, government offices, tribunals, temples, memorials and statues now stood in the area.

The weather was perfect for walking and sightseeing. April seemed to be a great month in Italy. Spring foliage had burst forth into a riot of greenery and flowers. You could smell it in the air around us. I wandered away from the group to savor the quiet. It seemed quite safe to do so. I kept our tour group in sight. People were everywhere, and the Colosseum stood as one big landmark. I couldn't get lost.

When I saw Maria use the red umbrella to gesture toward the bus, I made my way there.

I didn't rejoin Aunt Del and the others immediately. Bunny's voice got on my nerves a bit. So I wandered over to the wooden bench on the far side of the bus. Tony was standing there, smoking a cigarette. The bus hid him from the crowd.

"You caught me," he said, dropping the butt to the ground. I watched him stamp it out with his foot.

"Aha, so you're a smoker," I said, smiling.

"They don't like us to," said Tony. "It's a bad habit. I'm cutting down. I'm down to five a day."

"That's good. I know it's hard." I remembered when Rob had tried to quit. He had been miserable and had yelled a lot. Come to think of it, he had never been all that nice. Rob was one of those guys who complained all the time. Why had it taken me so long to see that?

Tony must have been reading my mind. "So...you're here with your aunt? Not with a husband or boyfriend?"

I started. "I just broke up with my long-time boyfriend three months ago."

"I'm sorry," said Tony.

"No. It's okay. *Now* it's okay. It wasn't at the time." I looked off into the bright blue sky. The sun was beaming lovely hot rays down on me. "We'd been together seven years. Ever since high school."

Tony kicked a pebble with the toe of his shoe. "If you want my opinion, your ex is an idiot."

"Thanks," I said softly. Three months earlier, I had thought I'd lost everything. Now it didn't seem to be quite so much. Maybe Italy did that to you. It made you see the good things in the world.

"Gentlemans and lovely ladies, please come here!" Rocco hollered.

Tony grinned at me. "Our fearless leader commands. We better move."

The ride back to the hotel was quiet. I figured everyone was still suffering from jet lag. Aunt Del suggested we have a rest until dinner. I didn't fight it. She set the alarm for seven o'clock. That would give us time to freshen up before going downstairs.

That night we had our first dinner as part of the tour. I was looking forward to the "Rustic Italian" menu. It was a specialty of the hotel. When we arrived in the dining room, Ed signaled us over.

"I made Ed come early to save seats for us," said Bunny. "He doesn't take any time to change his clothes."

Bunny obviously did. She was wearing a completely different outfit. Her electric-blue wraparound dress looked like it might have been featured in a magazine like *Vogue*. Everything Bunny wore screamed money, down to her diamond watch and designer shoes.

I was still wearing my aunt's parrot shirt. In some ways I matched the theme of the dining room. It was designed to be like an old conservatory or aviary. Small indoor trees were everywhere, and colorful birds graced the wallpaper. Arched windows faced a small courtyard. The effect was charming.

We started with an appetizer of freshly sliced tomatoes with basil leaves, balsamic vinegar and a soft cheese.

"That's mozzarella di bufala," explained Ed. "From water buffalos—not our North American kind. They farm them not far from Rome. We may see some along the roadside when we go to Sorrento tomorrow."

"It's delicious," I said, munching happily. Ed poured wine into our glasses. I thought it was generous of him to buy for the table.

Lovely aromas were coming from the kitchen. I could see a waiter walking to our table with plates of spaghetti.

"Mmmm...that smells good, even from this distance," I said.

It didn't smell so good ten seconds later when it landed on my shoulder.

The waiter started yelling in Italian. Ed translated it to "I don't know how that plate slipped from my hand!" I was pretty sure Ed had left out some other words.

Everyone fussed around me. I felt bad for the waiter, who couldn't stop wailing. The manager came over and began yelling and waving his arms around. Then the chef came out from the kitchen with both arms opened wide. He cried to the heavens as if he were in an opera. None of this helped very much. Unfortunately there wasn't much anyone could do about the tomato sauce running down my front.

"Another shirt bites the dust." Aunt Del picked a noodle out of my hair. "Why do things keep getting spilled on you and not me?"

I wondered the same thing.

"Good thing we're in the hotel," she said. "Go up and have a shower. I'll bring dinner up to you, and we'll call it a day."

As I stood up, a meatball slid to the floor.

Thank goodness for hot water. I lingered in the shower, enjoying every minute of it. I emailed Carrie when I got all cleaned up. I told her about the people on the tour and where we had gone.

The bus driver is very nice. His name is Tony. But you should see our tour guide, Rocco. Carrie, he's a dream! Movie-star good looks, and he's so friendly. I'll send you a photo tomorrow. We're leaving for Sorrento, with one stop along the way.

Still no sign of my luggage. Thank goodness I packed sandals in my carry-on!

Love from Rome,

Charlie

Eight

DAY THREE

"I have bad news," said Tony when I arrived at the bus the next morning. "Your suitcase is officially missing."

My mouth flew open. "But I thought it was in Australia!"

"It was," he said. "They supposedly sent it on the next flight to Italy. But it wasn't a direct flight. So it went via some other place. That's where it got lost, they think. I'm trying to find out where the stopover was. Might be in Asia. Might be in the other direction."

I let out a small giggle. "Well, I'm glad it's having a good time seeing the world. Sort of like one of those garden gnomes people take pictures of and post online. I hope someone puts stickers on my suitcase so we can see where it's been."

Tony smiled widely. "Now that's the spirit. You have to laugh when something like this happens."

He had a really nice smile. "There are worse things," I said, nodding. "At least I'm having a good time in Italy. Even if I do look like an escapee from the disco era."

He laughed. "Better that than from a retirement home. Your aunt has some pretty wild clothes."

Today I was wearing her hot-pink T-shirt with the big green parrot on it. I had knotted it at my waist to make it fit better. Even so, it slipped off one shoulder no matter what I did. Talk about 1980s!

It went perfectly with the sequined baseball cap she had given me.

"Hey, don't ruin my cover," I said. "I'm incognito on this trip." I slipped on my aunt's huge sunglasses. "Jackie Onassis, don't you think?" I struck a pose.

He chuckled again. "Before my time," he said. He looked up at me, and something in his face changed.

I did a spin for effect. The Italian sun beat down upon me. For the first time in a long time, it felt good to be alive.

Tony spoke softly. I couldn't be sure, but it sounded like he said, "I think you look perfect."

I turned back. "Sorry, what was that?"

"Nothing," he said. He looked away, toward Rocco and the hotel. Our tour was about to start.

Everyone crowded to the curb. I couldn't quite understood that. Our seating wasn't first-come, first choice. We all knew where we would be sitting today. One row back from yesterday. And yet people seemed to be anxious to get on first. Wanting that must be a human trait, I thought.

So Aunt Del and I sat in the second row today. Ed and Bunny were in the first.

Bunny and my aunt seemed to be competing for loudest outfit. Bunny had on a pink jean skirt and a pink T-shirt with silver sequins across it that spelled out *Bunny.*

"In case Ed forgets my name," she said, then giggled.

I didn't know how she'd managed to find that top. Or the matching silver sequined slip-on shoes.

My aunt wore a dazzling silk kimono top that had been hand-painted with sunset colors. Yellow, pink and mauve layers fell in panels like a stained-glass window. I would have worn black bottoms with that. She chose lime green.

I hid my eyes behind my borrowed sunglasses.

"This," said Rocco. He held up a candy bar for all of us to see. "This is the best sweet in the world. Yes, the entire world. It is soft nougat with almonds and honey." He kissed his fingers and swept them in the air. "You will buy this and think you are in heaven."

"I'll go to heaven if Rocco is there," said my aunt. Bunny burst into girlish laughter. Even Ed managed a smile.

Never boring, I reminded myself.

The trip from Rome to the historic town of Cassino took about two hours. Rocco shared a bit of history before we left the bus. The Abbey of Monte Cassino was originally built in the sixth century. It had to be rebuilt to repair damage after World War II. Now it was a regular stop for tourists traveling from Rome to Naples.

Our bus was one of many parked in diagonal rows designed for easy egress. That is a word I learned that day. It refers to the action of getting out.

We were encouraged to wander about. The views were stunning. I looked out from the Abbey terrace to the vista beyond. Everything one imagined Italy would be. Green vistas and hilly terrain. Vineyards off in the distance. Perfect—except for a very chilling sight. The cemeteries.

It was hard to take in that this had been the site of one of the bloodiest battles of World War II. Rocco had told us all about the final German defeat and horrific Allied losses.

In the bus I had listened politely. I couldn't have imagined the impact that seeing this would have on me.

It took a while for the sadness to pass. Then I remembered that much was still to come on this trip. It was the ancient Romans who intrigued me most. I was excited that I'd be seeing Pompeii in two days.

We had a quick lunch at the canteen. I thoroughly enjoyed my sandwich of fresh tomato, basil and mozzarella di bufala. In fact, I could possibly get addicted to this combination. Even better, none of it ended up on my clothes.

Aunt Del wanted to use the washroom "one last time." So I wandered over to the lookout. Tony was standing there.

"My grandfather was at the battle of Monte Cassino," he said. "He never talked about it. Makes you think, seeing the place for real."

Just what I had been mulling earlier. All those young lives lost. Many of them younger than we were now. "I'm trying to imagine what this place looked like with all the men in uniform," I said.

I looked at Tony. He was wearing a uniform of sorts. Navy pants and a navy golf shirt with the company crest. His golf hat had the same crest. I guessed that was so we tourists could find him easily. Rocco wore the same thing.

"So tell me," I said. "You know a lot of history. Why aren't you the tour guide instead of the bus driver?"

Tony glanced at me. "People don't realize how much skill it takes to drive a bus. Especially through narrow roads like they have here."

"I didn't mean to criticize," I said quickly. "I just meant—"

He smiled then. "I know what you meant. Being a tour guide looks glamorous. The ladies fall all over you. I don't like being onstage like that. I'm better one on one."

I felt awful. I had made it sound like Rocco's job was more important than Tony's. And it wasn't true. Bus drivers kept us safe. How could I have been so insensitive? Why didn't I stop to think before I spoke?

"Probably I should be getting back to the bus," he said.

We had to weave our way through another tour group coming in. Most of the men and some of the women towered over me, and I got jostled. I didn't even see the person who spilled soda pop down my arm.

"Was that hot?" Tony's voice held concern.

"No, thank goodness," I said. "It's cola, not coffee. Yuck. It's sticky."

Tony pulled a tissue from his pocket and handed it to me. I tried to mop up the liquid, but the fabric was soaked.

"Oh no, there's a bee!" I yelled. And another! Tony tried to swat it away with his golf hat. But then another came at me.

"Run for the bus!" Tony said. He grabbed my hand, and we dashed across the parking lot. Tony had the bus door open in no time. He pushed me up the steps and then vaulted up himself, closing the door behind him.

"Any hangers-on?" he said.

"I can't see any." I laughed out loud. "We left them bee-hind," I said.

He chuckled with me. "Next time we'll bee more wary," he said. "Bee-lieve me."

I groaned.

Other passengers started to line up, so Tony opened the door. When Aunt Del sat down beside me, I was still smiling.

Aunt Del spotted my soggy arm immediately. "What happened?" she said.

I told her.

"You've got to be more careful, Charlie," she said. "I'm running out of tops."

I burst out laughing again.

When everyone was aboard, we headed for our next destination—Sorrento. We were staying there three nights. Saturday, Sunday and Monday. This was our gateway to the Amalfi Coast. Just off the shore from Sorrento was the famous island of Capri. We would be seeing that on Monday.

Aunt Del and I were seated in the second row, so I couldn't talk to Rocco across the aisle anymore. Bunny and Ed were still in front of us. Bunny turned around to talk to my aunt every now and then. I just smiled, happy that Aunt Del had found a friend on the trip.

"Don't forget it's dress-up night tonight," said Bunny at one point. "Rocco told me even the staff go all out, being Italian and all. Has Charlie got anything to wear?"

Rats! That was something I hadn't thought of after being told my luggage was lost. Wearing oversized tops during the day was one thing. But they would never do for a dress-up dinner.

"Fiddlesticks," said Aunt Del, looking over at me. "I brought two dresses with me, but they'd fall right off her."

"I may have something," said Bunny. "I brought lots of clothes. Leave it with me."

"That's very nice of you," I said, choking back horror. It was one thing to borrow my aunt's clothes. We all knew she was crazy for color. But Bunny? She dressed like she was about to go clubbing. Even during the day. And then I remembered my new mantra. Why be boring? Whatever Bunny had, it wouldn't be boring.

Nine

I was right about that. When we'd settled into our rooms, Bunny came bouncing through the door with something draped over her arm.

"This dress is a bit snug. You're smaller than me, so it should fit you. It's knee length on me, and it won't matter if it's longer on you. What do you think?"

She held up a sleek leopard-print dress with a deep V neck and bars of sequins on the shoulders. It had a sequined belt that fastened at the back. I couldn't hold in my giggle.

"See, Della? She likes it!" Bunny held it out to me. "This will look great on you, Charlie. You'll wow them."

No doubt about it. If I were in the jungle, I'd wow Tarzan for sure. But I accepted it graciously and locked myself in the bathroom to try it on. One look in the bathroom mirror sent me into another fit of giggles.

"I was right!" cried Bunny when I returned. She clapped her hands. "It fits you like a dream. You can keep it, Charlie. It's really too small for me, and I brought lots. Doesn't she look great, Della?"

My aunt smiled, and her blue eyes twinkled. "She does indeed. Definitely not boring."

I felt like I was playing dress-up in the wardrobe department of a movie studio. No way would I wear anything like this in real life. But this trip wasn't real life, I reasoned. I thanked her profusely.

"Whoops, I better get going," said Bunny, looking at her sparkly watch. "I need to do something with my hair and get dressed. See you downstairs at eight."

People in Italy ate dinner late. We were meeting for drinks first, but dinner wouldn't be until nine, I knew. I just hoped I'd make it through the meal without food ending up on me.

Tony wouldn't be there. He never joined us for meals. Bus drivers didn't, I was told. The company wouldn't pay for it. But as our tour guide, Rocco always had dinner with us. I wondered what he would think of my dress.

I looked around the room for a mirror. There was a long one behind the door. I took a quick look at myself. A little lipstick and mascara was all I really needed. The sun had given my face some nice color.

Then I walked over to the bed closest to the door. This room was a more modern copy of our first one back in Rome. Maybe a few feet longer, with sliding glass doors leading to a small balcony. I loved the color scheme of soft yellow and blue. These weren't the bright colors of Aunt Del's wardrobe. It was like they had been left out in the Italian sun and had faded to something cozy.

I sat on the bed and slipped on my sandals.

"What do you think...purple or orange?" Aunt Del had two dresses laid out on her bed.

"Purple," I said firmly. "It looks great with your dark hair."

"Are you sure? It's a little dull." She frowned at it.

Dull? The purple dress had a flouncy, tiered skirt. The neckline was cut pretty darn low. "Why did you buy it if you think it's dull?" I asked.

"Well, you never know when you might have to go to a funeral," she said.

I stared at her. "What kind of funerals do you go to?"

She laughed along with me.

"Maybe if I throw some jewelry on..." she said.

"Do that," I said. "More bling never hurts." Gad, I was starting to sound more like my aunt every day.

Since I was already dressed, I told her to meet me downstairs. I wanted to see the views of the ocean from the hotel terrace. That was true. But I also hoped Rocco might be there before the others.

I raced down the stairs to the main lobby. Crystal chandeliers sparkled in the dining room before me. I paused for a bit, admiring the lovely reception rooms. Both of our hotels on this trip had been beautiful. Just the right mix of old-world charm and modern convenience. I turned right to go out the double glass doors to the terrace overlooking the ocean.

I was not disappointed. The view was stunning. I leaned right up against the fancy wrought-iron railing. The golden sun was beginning to set, but even so I could see the gorgeous bright blue of the water. It was a different color from the lakes back home. You could imagine this sea teaming with life.

I stared at the Gulf of Naples for several minutes, drinking in the warm, humid air. The weather on our trip had been perfect so far. Always warm without being stifling. I felt like a weight was starting to lift off me. Italy did that to you, I decided.

When a hand fell on my shoulder, I turned. Rocco didn't disappoint. He was dressed in a black tux with a white frilly shirt that was open at the neck. Curly black chest hair peeked out.

"You look ravishing, Sharlie," he said. I loved the way he pronounced my name. No one else said it like that. He reached for my hand and kissed the back of it. I felt chills. Then he took the same hand in both of his. I felt him put a note in it. He curled my fingers around it.

"My room number," he said quietly. "Tomorrow. In the afternoon. We can talk away from the others. And share a drink or two."

He looked right into my eyes, and his smile was dazzling.

"Rocco!" someone called. He turned away from me to meet one of the other guests.

I returned to the lobby to wait for my aunt. Bunny and Ed came down almost immediately, then Aunt Del. We shared a table in the glitzy dining room. I was in a daze the whole night. I ate my five-course dinner with enthusiasm, hardly noticing what the others were saying.

All I could think was that Rocco wanted to see me alone! How wonderful was that? *Guess I wasn't boring after all.*

After dinner people got up to dance. Before long Aunt Del had everyone doing the twist. I tried to follow her moves, but she kept coming up with something new. Before long I had to kick off my sandals. When the music switched to disco, she was in her element.

"I'm not doing the bump," I said firmly.

"Yes you are." She grabbed my arm and dragged me to the middle of the dance floor.

I'm not sure I can describe what happened next. Apparently, I'm not very good at the bump.

From my vantage point on the floor, I could see the overhead chandeliers clearly. I could also see a ring of faces staring down into mine. I fought for air.

"Are you okay?" said a male voice.

I was clearly not okay. I was splayed on the floor and could not move.

"Fine!" I yelled up into the faces. "I'm fine!"

A crowd had gathered. Not the sort of crowd that gently lifts you off the ground. More the sort of crowd that gawks.

"Wow, that must have hurt," said someone helpfully.

No shit, Sherlock.

"Someone help her up," said my aunt. Now we got action. Two older men took hold of me under my arms and lifted me to my feet. I tested each limb for damage. Luckily, the only thing that seemed to be broken was my pride. I looked around for Rocco, but he was nowhere to be seen. I was glad of that.

"Are you sure you're okay?" asked Aunt Del.

"Yes," I said. I think we were all grateful when a slow song come on.

Later, as we were getting ready for bed, Aunt Del noticed my smile. "You look happy, Charlie. I'm glad."

"I *am* happy," I said, pulling the leopard-print dress over my head. I was glad to see it had survived the great fall without any damage. Oddly enough, no one had thrown food on it either.

"Thanks for bringing me on this trip, Aunt Del," I said. "It's been wonderful for me."

She put her hand on my arm. "Seeing you happy again is the best thing in the world for me."

I turned to hug her. She really was the best aunt in the world. Even if she did dance like a wild thing.

It was after two a.m. when I emailed Carrie. I told her almost everything about the night. I wasn't sure why, but I left out the part about Rocco giving me the note.

I do have good news, Carrie. You'll be happy to hear I'm getting over Rob. I went the whole day without thinking about him once. I think the

Italian cure is working. Wish you could be here, and someday, we *will* find a way. I promise! Maybe we can take an ocean liner across the Atlantic to Italy. Wouldn't that be fun?

 Love from Sorrento,

 Charlie

Ten

The next morning I got up earlier than my aunt, as usual. We'd had a late night, so it wasn't all that early, to be honest. Okay, it was closer to lunch than breakfast. We were on our own for both meals today, so I was relieved to skip one. It was cheaper that way.

I dressed quietly in the flouncy white peasant blouse she had left out for me. It had red lace trim and no parrots. I knotted the hem around my waist. Then I dashed downstairs. The hotel had both a dining room and a café. I grabbed a quick sandwich and cappuccino in the cheaper café and hurried out to the street. We had the whole day free for exploring and shopping in Sorrento. I intended to find something special for Rocco.

It was a shame I was so limited by money. But what I was looking for wouldn't cost the earth.

Sorrento is a coastal town, facing the Bay of Naples. The town is perched atop cliffs that separate it from the busy marinas below. You can't beat the sweeping water views.

On our way to the hotel the day before, we had driven down a side street with shops. It was only a block away. The main town square was about a mile farther down that same street. Probably I could get what I wanted in the first block.

Our hotel was close to the ocean, so I had to walk uphill to get to the side street. It wasn't all that busy. I spotted a small shop of specialty foods and entered.

A middle-aged man wearing an apron was arguing with a pretty teenage girl who looked to be his daughter. She yelled something to him in Italian, and he yelled back. Arms waved with a language all their own. She burst into tears and then stomped out of the place. I moved swiftly out of her way to avoid being whacked.

"Eye-yi-yi!" the shopkeeper cried to the heavens, with his arms in the air. Then he noticed me and smiled sheepishly. "Englese?" he said.

I nodded. "American."

"We fight, my daughter. Her boyfriend— eh! No like him." He shook his head violently and continued to mutter in Italian.

I walked up to the candy counter, determined to complete my mission. There it was! The exact type of nougat Rocco had shown us on the bus. He'd said it was the best, so I knew he must like it. I picked it up and handed it to the owner.

"This is delizioso," he said, handing me change. "For you? Or for special person?"

I was grinning from ear to ear as I left the little store.

When I got back to the room, Aunt Del was struggling to get dressed.

"It's a beautiful day," I said, bouncing in. "I want to explore all over town."

Aunt Del groaned. "I think you'll be doing it alone, sweetie. I can hardly move this morning, after all that dancing last night. Think it will be a quiet day on the patio for me."

"Maybe a massage would help," I suggested. She really did look as if every movement pained her.

"I'll look into that. Don't worry about me. I'm going to take it easy and rest up for Pompeii tomorrow."

"Are you sure?" I didn't want to leave her if she was in real pain.

She smiled at me. "You have a nice day

checking out the shops and sites. I'll meet you back on the patio at six."

I hated to see Aunt Del in pain. But it really was awfully convenient timing. I had plans for the afternoon, and I didn't want her to know about them.

◊ ◊ ◊

Rocco had said afternoon. I waited until one o'clock. His room was on the ground floor, on the side of the hotel that didn't have an ocean view. I found it easily.

I knocked tentatively on the door. There seemed to be some noise coming from the room. Maybe Rocco had the television on and couldn't hear me.

I knocked more loudly.

There was a pause in the noise from within. I put my ear up to the door. Then a sleepy voice sang out.

"Who is it, Rocco?"

Bunny Hopper's voice! The nougat dropped from my hand.

"Tell them to go away," she said.

I didn't wait a second. I dashed down the hall and around the corner. I fled to the stairs. At the bottom I turned right and headed for the patio doors. Once outside, my eyes welled with tears.

What a fool I had been!

Of course I'd known Rocco would have other girlfriends. He was so good-looking. And charming. Probably he had girlfriends in every city, I thought bitterly. But Bunny Hopper! She was married. How could he do that? Not only that, she had to be about twenty years older than him.

I remembered what Tony had said about being a tour guide. *The ladies fall all over you.* Obviously I wasn't the only one Rocco had given a note to. I wasn't special after all.

Someone had come up behind me. "Charlie? Are you okay?" Tony's voice was low.

He joined me at the railing. I wiped my eyes with the back of my hand. But it was no use. He could tell I was upset.

"I saw you race out here," Tony said quietly. "Thinking about your ex, I guess."

After a pause I nodded. I'd let him think that. It was a much better story than the real one. The real story was too depressing.

"Please don't let one man ruin your holiday," he said.

I nearly laughed out loud. It was one man. But not the one Tony was thinking of.

Time to snap out of it, I told myself. After all, I had wanted adventures on this trip. You had to expect bad ones as well as good ones.

I found my smile again. "No man is going to ruin anything for me. I love Italy. This trip has been good for me." And I meant it.

"It's great, isn't it?" His voice was full of excitement. "And tomorrow you'll see Pompeii. It's amazing. Sometimes you can actually feel the ghosts who roam around there. At least, I can."

I looked at him curiously. "I wouldn't have thought you were such a romantic."

"You mean such a crackpot." He chuckled. "Funny. I've dated a lot of girls, and none of them ever called me a romantic. But I admit it. These ancient ruins really get me. All those lives lived before ours. People having families, going about their business, working hard every day. It makes you think."

"Yes, it does," I said. "Which reminds me. You don't have to answer this if you don't want to. I'm just curious. What did you do in Chicago before you became a tour-bus driver in Italy? I've been trying to guess."

"Elementary, my dear Watson." His eyes twinkled at me. "I drove a bus."

Eleven

"**What are you** doing for the rest of the day?" asked Tony. The strong sunlight streamed down over his shoulder, nearly blinding me.

"Nothing much," I said, using my hand to shade my eyes. "I'm on my own. Aunt Del wants to rest up for Pompeii tomorrow. She kind of overdid it last night."

Tony smiled. "I heard. Nobody had ever seen anyone do the twist like that."

I smiled too. Aunt Del had brought down the house, as usual. Everyone had stopped to watch and clap. At least she hadn't done cartwheels.

"If you want to go into town, I'll walk with you. I have to check in at the tour office to pick up things for tomorrow." He pushed back from the railing.

"Sure," I said. "Is it really true they have fan stores here? I mean, stores that sell nothing but fans?" I was determined to buy a souvenir for Carrie. A beautiful fan would be perfect. Maybe I could buy one for each of us.

"You'll see," he said.

I followed Tony across the patio and up the stone steps that would lead us to town.

◊ ◊ ◊

They really did have fan stores. And stores for ceramics. The town was also famous for its locally made lacework. And a type of wood mosaic called marquetry. Beautiful old shops led to the Piazza Tasso, which was lined with cafés.

"Nice, huh," said Tony. "But first let me take you to the historic center. I want to show you the Chiesa di San Francesco."

Tony took me down a warren of narrow alleys that led us to a tiny fourteenth-century church.

"It's Franciscan. The first time I came here, I almost walked by it," he said. "The exterior doors were so dark and foreboding."

"It's spectacular," I said as we entered. "Serene and tranquil." I loved the pretty ceiling. It wasn't heavy dark wood, like so many early churches. Instead light streamed in and reflected off the gold vaulted ceiling. Each vault was trimmed with white. But there was something else I liked about it. So many Italian churches were ornate to the point of overwhelming. This church from the 1500s was beautiful without being gaudy.

A young man and woman were talking to the priest at the front, before the altar.

It looked like they were discussing where to stand for a wedding.

"We don't have to stay long," Tony said quietly, taking my arm. "I just wanted you to see it." We went back outside to the well-kept gardens. Everything was bursting with flowers.

"What is that gorgeous smell?" I asked.

"Wisteria, mimosa, jasmine...take your pick. Spring is terrific in Sorrento. It gets really hot in summer. Look—there's a lemon tree." Tony pointed to a tree laden with fruit.

"Lots of English people get married here," he said. We stood still, looking at the pretty facade of the church.

"I don't blame them," I said. "It's perfect."

We retraced our steps through the alleys. Tony was quiet on the way back. I wondered if he hoped to get married at that church someday. Then I wondered if one of those girls he'd dated had let him down. It wasn't the sort of thing I felt comfortable asking about.

When we got back to the piazza, it was bustling. "If you are going to buy anything here, it should be a fan," said Tony. "Sorrento is famous for them. And they aren't too expensive."

"That's a plus," I said. I had to watch my euros like a hawk now. So far I had held off using my credit card. I really shouldn't be adding to the balance already on there.

"I need to get to the tour office now. Can you find your way back to the hotel? You just need to go that way." He pointed to the street that led to our hotel.

"No problem," I said. "I have a good sense of direction." Okay, that was a slight exaggeration. I'd never actually tested it in a strange place.

But it turned out I didn't need to worry.

I bought two gorgeous fans in one store. Both were black with hand-painted flowers and edged in black lace. In the store next door I found an inexpensive turquoise scoop-neck T-shirt that said *Sorrento* on it. I would wear that for Pompeii. Aunt Del had been so kind, lending me her clothes. Especially since they'd ended up getting trashed. Nevertheless, it would be a relief to wear something that actually fit me well.

I killed another hour looking in shop windows. One day I would come back with more money, I promised myself. Then I slowly began the journey back to the hotel.

Twelve

When I arrived at the hotel, I got a surprise. Aunt Del was sitting on the patio. It was impossible to miss her because she was wearing the same colorful hand-painted top from the day before. I felt slightly guilty. She must have been rationing her remaining clean clothes, since I was going through so many of them.

Thing is, she wasn't alone. A middle-aged man sat across from her. I recognized him from the bus, but we hadn't met yet.

She waved me over. "Charlie! Over here."

The man stood up as I approached. You didn't see that every day. Aunt Del made the introductions. "Charlie, this is Sam Conti. He lives in Hamilton, over the border in Canada."

"Not far from you," he said. We shook hands. He was heavyset but pleasant-looking, with thick gray hair and brown eyes that twinkled.

"What brings you here?" I asked. Okay, I was being nosy. It was obvious Aunt Del liked him, and I didn't want an absent wife to suddenly appear. The experience with Rocco had spooked me. Best to be prepared.

"My parents were from Italy, but I'd never been," said Sam. "I always wanted to come here with my wife. She died two years ago."

"I'm sorry," I said. "So you came alone?" I couldn't help probing. Just call me Sherlock.

He gave me a warm smile. "This trip is my way of starting over. Remember the past fondly, but live in the present."

"I like that," said Aunt Del. "Remember the past, but live in the present. What do you think, Charlie?"

"I think that's the wisest thing I've ever heard," I said.

Sam excused himself to "freshen up," as my aunt would say. The second he left, I could tell she had something important to tell me.

"Look, Charlie," she blurted out. "I don't want to interfere. But I've just got to say it. Don't fall for Rocco."

I nearly fell off my chair. "Don't worry. I haven't. I think he's fully occupied anyway."

She gave me a low chuckle. "Yes, he's already bagged a rabbit."

I stared at her. *Bagged a rabbit*. "Bunny Hopper! How did you know?"

"Sweetie, that woman couldn't stick to one man if they used superglue. And Rocco is gorgeous. I'm sure her vacation wouldn't be complete unless she'd managed to cheat on poor Ed with at least one schmuck." Aunt Del sipped from her wineglass. "And the sad thing is, I'm sure he knows it. Puts up with it because she brings sparkle into his life."

"How strange," I said. "I could never settle for a marriage like that."

"Neither could I," she said. "Luckily I didn't have to."

Thirteen

When Sam returned, we went in to dinner. I was grateful for his company, to be honest. In a totally selfish way. I didn't want to sit with Ed and Bunny. I didn't think I could look at her without giving away what I knew.

Sam had the same thought about privacy, I could see. The table he chose would fit only three. I actually enjoyed dinner that night. The food was delicious—fresh fish (from the ocean right out front) in a savory lemon and caper sauce. Yummy chocolate gelato for dessert. I spilled only a little bit on my peasant blouse. The rest landed on my yoga pants.

Sam insisted on calling the waiter over to bring me another serving. Aunt Del assured me that gelato would wash out of my pants.

Sam had bought a nice crisp wine for the table. We toasted the future. I enjoyed watching him and Aunt Del talk. He seemed taken with her. I could understand that. Life was never boring when Aunt Del was around.

I thought it would be nice if she had a gentleman friend. Hamilton was only an hour from Buffalo. It could be workable.

By the time espresso came, I was completely relaxed. Who knew what adventure the next day would bring? I would be ready for it.

When we got back to the room, I washed my yoga pants in the sink. I'd worn the poor things every day of the trip, so they needed a good wash anyway. It was a warm night. Aunt Del suggested I drape the pants over one of the chairs on the balcony. "They'll be dry by morning," she said.

After that I emailed Carrie. I didn't even mention Rocco.

Guess what? It looks like Aunt Del may have found a gentleman friend. I came back from shopping (yes, I bought you something!!) and she was sitting with a man about her age. He seems nice and lives about an hour away from Buffalo.

I know you hoped something romantic would happen for me on this trip, Carrie. Well, it looks like it will happen to Aunt Del instead.

Love from Sorrento,

Charlie

Fourteen

DAY FIVE

The next morning disaster struck.

"Oh no!" I cried from the balcony.

"What's wrong?" asked Aunt Del, still in her nightgown.

"My pants!" They were not on the chair. They were not on the balcony floor. I couldn't even see them anywhere on the ground below. Nor on the road leading up to the town square.

Aunt Del dashed to my side. "Uh-oh," she said. "A wind must have come up in the night." She gazed off into the distance. "I wonder where they flew to?"

I groaned. First my suitcase had gone on a trip of its own. Now my only pair of pants was doing the same thing.

"What am I going to wear?" I wailed. This was serious now. The only clothes I had were the things in Aunt Del's suitcase. Plus the T-shirt I'd bought the day before. A few tops and no bottoms.

"I know!" said Aunt Del. "Wear the dress Bunny gave you with the T-shirt you bought yesterday over top. That way the dress will look like a skirt."

And the gaudy shoulder sequins would be covered up. "Good idea," I said.

"It's only for one day," she said. "We can go shopping tomorrow, when we have free time."

"This is going to look crazy with running shoes," I said. But I had to wear running shoes. We would be walking all day at Pompeii, and my sandals were too strappy.

"Who cares?" said Aunt Del. "It might even look chic."

It did not look chic. I was wearing leopard print on the bottom, and a turquoise T-shirt with lettering on top. My hat was hot pink with sequins. My running shoes were black and lime green.

"Em…for sure we'll go shopping tomorrow," said Aunt Del.

I sighed. Apparently there was a limit to "Why be boring?" I picked up my shoulder bag.

The good news continued when I got to the bus.

"Toledo?" I couldn't believe it. "My bag is in Toledo? Isn't that in Spain?"

"Actually…" Tony hesitated. "I think they meant the Toledo in Ohio. I expect the baggage tag ripped off. These things happen."

Ohio, I thought. My baggage was nearly home, and so were all my clothes.

"Rats," I said, throwing my arms in the air. "I'm seriously running out of things to wear."

Tony looked down at my outfit and grinned. "I kind of thought so."

I felt my cheeks blush. "So. Toledo," I said.

"Yup. Nice place. I've been there," he said.

"Really?" It didn't seem like the sort of place you would go to unless you had a reason to.

"Yeah. I took a gap year between high school and college. Traveled around to find myself."

I'd always found that expression funny. "And did you? Find yourself?"

He shook his head. "I don't think that's how it works. Or, at least, it didn't for me. I would have been better off going directly to college. Then I might have finished."

"I didn't go to college," I said. "My family didn't have the money, and I was needed at the deli." I told Tony about Carrie and the care she required.

"That must be tough," said Tony. "How much younger is she?"

"Seven years," I said. For some reason I started to choke up. "I'd do anything for her. She's the best little sister in the world."

I could feel Tony's eyes on me. "I'm sure she says the same about her older sister."

I wanted to ask more about him. Like what he had been studying and why he didn't finish. But the others were upon us.

"Buon giorno, peoples! Hurry to the bus. We go to Pompeii today." Rocco's voice soared through the air.

It was strange. The voice that had so captivated me before seemed different now. Too high for a man.

We were later starting out today. It was Sunday, and the hotel had provided a lovely brunch as part of the tour package. Sam had joined us for breakfast. I was happy to see he had scooped the same table for three.

As well, the tour company had allowed time for people to go to church if they desired. This was Italy, after all. So it was almost noon by the time the bus pulled out of the parking lot.

Aunt Del and I were in the third row now. I was secretly relieved to be well back from Rocco. I didn't think he would know it had been me at the door the previous afternoon. At least, he couldn't be sure. If I kept my distance, he would never know.

It was impossible to avoid Ed and Bunny, however. They were still seated directly in front of us. Bunny was delighted to see me wearing her dress. "Well, what do you know?" she said. "I never thought to wear it as a skirt."

"It's all the rage in Paris," said Aunt Del. I choked back a laugh.

When we got underway, Bunny continued

to talk to my aunt as usual. I smiled weakly and kept my thoughts to myself.

Bunny pulled something out of her huge handbag. "Have some of this delicious nougat before I eat it all up," she said. She handed it back to my aunt.

I almost yelped out loud. It looked like the same bar of nougat I had dropped outside Rocco's door!

I was so tempted to ask where Bunny had gotten it. My aunt ripped a piece off and offered it to me. I shook my head. She must have wondered at the wide grin on my face.

◊ ◊ ◊

Hot. Dry. Glorious. Those were the words that came to mind while I gazed upon the ancient ruins of Pompeii.

I stayed with Aunt Del throughout the basic group tour. It took about two hours.

No question, the visit to Pompeii was the highlight of our trip to Italy. Anyone's trip to Italy, I would bet.

Our tour guide told us the basics. We learned that the whole city of Pompeii was completely buried under ash and pumice when Mount Vesuvius erupted in AD 79. The objects that had lain beneath the ash had been preserved for more than a thousand years because of lack of air and moisture. I could see why Pompeii was so special. All the things that were dug up provided incredible details about everyday life during the Roman era. Now visitors like us could wander through the streets and houses that had been excavated, including the Villa of Mysteries. You could even see Vesuvius in the distance, which was spooky.

But there was something enchanting about Pompeii. I wanted to experience it by myself, without the distraction of people chattering.

Rocco had given us a time to meet back at the bus. I quietly detached myself from the group and left to explore the side streets alone. I didn't intend to go far.

As I wandered down the ancient streets, something in me woke up. With a start, I realized that I was happy. The misty weight had lifted. I no longer cared about Rob. I no longer wondered what he was doing every minute. The Italian cure had worked.

It wasn't just the sunshine. The people in Italy seemed to radiate a zest for life. It wasn't only their love of food and beautiful things. They seemed to thrive in the company of other people. Even when they argued—which they did often—they did it with gusto.

My solitary walk brought me to an intersection. I turned and looked down the stone road ahead. A beautiful ancient fountain stood not far away. The Romans had loved fountains. They were all over Rome. This one in Pompeii had no water running anymore, of course. But the sun was shining in a way that made it seem magical. I dug in my shoulder bag for my cell phone, so I could take a photo.

I was just framing the fountain for a picture when it happened. I heard a snip and felt a tug. Someone had cut the back strap of my shoulder bag!

"My purse!" I yelled.

Fifteen

The phone dropped from my hand. A man took off down the side street with my bag. I set off after him, running as fast as I could. He whipped around a corner, and I followed. Down a long cobblestone lane we raced. I didn't bother yelling. I couldn't spare a breath.

What to do? He was pulling ahead of me. On and on we ran. Obviously he was young and fit. Taller than me, with longer legs, and used to running on cobblestones. Even with my running shoes, I didn't stand a chance of catching him.

He turned another corner. When I got there, he was nowhere to be seen.

I stopped, panting hard. I leaned over to catch my breath. When I straightened, I saw that he had led me to a large public square. Many deserted lanes converged on it. I didn't have a hope of knowing which one he'd gone down.

In front of me, in the middle of the square, was a temple. The roof was gone, but two-thousand-year-old marble columns stood proudly in the sun.

I inhaled big gulps of air. Then I climbed up the steps to the top of the temple for the best view. The rotten thief was nowhere in sight. No one was in sight. I was miles away from where I had started. I didn't even have my phone. Which way should I go? So much for the good sense of direction I had boasted to Tony about.

The sun was beating down brutally. It didn't seem friendly anymore. Beautiful

Pompeii had turned into a scary place of robbers and ghosts.

I sat down on the stone platform, feeling defeated. There was no sense running around in circles. Best to stay in one place and be visible. My heart was still beating fiercely. What could I do to calm down?

Without my phone, I couldn't even write to Carrie. But oh, what a tale I would have to tell her when this was all over. That's the spirit, I told myself. You will get back to the hotel.

Of course I would. Pompeii was a tourist site. Some tour guide or employee would come by eventually. Aunt Del would miss me. They would send a search party. Wouldn't they? I felt a jolt of fear.

Time passed. I wasn't wearing a watch, so I couldn't tell how much. Thankfully, I still had my hat. And I was wearing a colorful T-shirt. On this temple platform I would be easy to see from anywhere in the square. All I had to do was wait patiently and not get sunstroke.

If only I wasn't so lousy at being patient.

I started to think about what I would tell Carrie. In my mind I was already writing the email. I would tell her about the ruins. How life had stood still in Pompeii. I would tell her about the loaves of bread found in the ancient bakery ovens. How there were grooves in the road made by chariot wheels. How people in Pompeii decorated their walls with colorful murals. You could still see them in the Vettii Villa. It made the past seem real, what I had seen today. So many people just like us, living their everyday lives. So many people who didn't make it out of Pompeii when Vesuvius erupted.

I could see Vesuvius clearly from where I sat on the temple platform. A little sob escaped me. I could, in that moment, imagine how they felt.

And that's how Tony found me. Sitting on the top step of the temple, imagining how it would have been for all those people in those last moments. I heard him calling my name from far away. I called back. I stood up so Tony could see me. And then he was around the corner, coming fast. He ran up the temple steps. When he opened his arms, it was the most natural thing in the world to fall into them.

His forehead was sweaty. His heart was beating hard. Of course, it was Tony. I should have seen it all along. Rocco wasn't real. He was what you imagined was the perfect guy. Not the real thing at all.

The real thing was the man who went looking for you when you were lost.

"A thief stole my purse," I said into his chest. "I tried to chase him and ran for ages. Then I couldn't find my way back."

"I thought it might be that," said Tony

into my hair. "Is your passport in the hotel safe?"

I nodded.

"Then don't worry. It's just a purse. You won't see it again, I'm afraid. But we can replace anything in it." He kissed the top of my head.

Luckily, I didn't have much money in the purse. Turned out to be a good thing I came with so little. The poor robber would be disappointed. Life is funny like that.

"Don't go home yet," Tony said, releasing me.

"What?" All I wanted to do was get back to the hotel. But that wasn't what he meant.

"Stay an extra week. Please." He was pacing now. "Look. I don't know where this is going to go. But I don't want you to walk away before we find out. I'll pay for your flight home. I have money. And I can put you up with my aunt. She has an extra room."

"Tony, what are you saying?" I asked. This was crazy talk. My heart was beating like a jungle drum.

He stopped pacing. "No. That's too much to expect. I'm an idiot. Let me think." He ran a hand through his hair. "How about this. You go back home. I'm due for some time off. I can take a vacation back to the States to visit my parents. I could go to Buffalo for a few days. See you there."

I felt stunned. He'd do that for me?

Tony went on. "And then—if you wanted me to—I could stay. I can go back to the States to work. I will if you want me to. But let me visit you there. And then we'll see."

"But you have to work—"

"I'm owed a week off. They'll let me take it." He held out his arms. "Please, Charlie. Let me visit you there. See where this goes. I've been restless for so long. Then you came here, and it was like the sun came out."

No one, ever, had said words like that to me. I walked into his arms. When they wrapped around me, I felt breathless. My heart soared with happiness.

It came back to me then. Aunt Del's saying. *With every end comes a new beginning.*

"Of course I want you to come to Buffalo. But—oh, Tony!" I said, pushing back. "What am I going to tell Aunt Del?"

"I don't think you have to worry about her. In fact, she may be something of a witch."

"How so?" I asked.

He smiled. "When I left the tour group just now, I promised her I was going to find you. Your aunt gave me a funny look and said, 'Yes. I'm sure you will. And she'll find you too.'"

I gazed up into his warm brown eyes. "She was right," I said.

AUTHOR'S NOTE

This book is born of love. It shimmers with my love for Italy, where we still have family. How I enjoyed going back with my mother to the places described in this story. Those places sing in my memory.

More love: I lost my husband, Dave, to cancer this year. He was one in a million. No one could have been more supportive to me as an author. All through the writing of this book, I was remembering the way our love began. In the last chapter, you will read this: "Then you came here, and it was like the sun came out." Dave said that to me long, long ago. In all the years since, it has seemed to me the most beautiful thing a man could say to a woman. Charlie feels that way too.

ACKNOWLEDGMENTS

It isn't often a crime writer gets asked to write romantic comedy. So I have a few people to thank.

First up, a big thank-you to readers who enthused about *Worst Date Ever*, my first rom-com with Orca Book Publishers. You made me realize that I could do to romance what I do to crime—that is, blow it out of the water with loopy comedy.

Second, a hearty thanks to the friends who encourage that wacky side of me: Cathy Astolfo, Janet Bolin, Alison Bruce, Cheryl Freedman, Don Graves, Jeannette Harrison, Joan O'Callaghan and Nancy O'Neil.

Finally, I am forever grateful to Ruth Linka and her team, who not only publish my books, but make them better. This is book number ten with Orca. Count me grateful.

Winner of 10 awards, MELODIE CAMPBELL has been both a finalist for and a winner of the Derringer and Arthur Ellis Awards for crime writing. She has over two hundred publications, including a hundred comedy credits, forty short stories and several books in the Rapid Reads collection, including the Goddaughter series. Her work has appeared in *Alfred Hitchcock Mystery Magazine*, *Star Magazine*, *Flash Fiction Magazine*, *Canadian Living*, the *Toronto Star*, the *Globe and Mail* and many more. Melodie lives in Oakville, Ontario.

9781459815599 · $9.95 PB

ONE

One day I am going to write a book. It is going to be called *A Dummy's Guide to Men*. It will include all sorts of useful tips, such as how to find Prince Charming in a sea of Prince Ronalds.

I am well qualified to write about this subject. This is because I have recently met a lot of Prince Ronalds. I met them all through an online dating site. I blame my friend Angela for pushing me into online dating. She also gave me the idea for the book. It started like this…

"You signed up?" said Angela. She plunked down onto the plastic chair opposite me.

I nodded. "Yup. E-Galaxy, here I come."

"It's time." Angela cradled her coffee mug with both hands. "It's been two years, Jennie. Two years since Greg died. It's time you started dating."

She could say his name now without me bursting into tears. So I guess time had done some healing. But it had been such a shock. Who expects their husband to die of a heart attack at thirty-four?

I forced the thought from my mind and instead filled my mouth with coffee.

It was Sunday evening. We were seated in the Original Coffeehouse, a cute little coffee bistro on Main. It was close to my new apartment. Angela said they had the best coffee in town. Better than the chains.

It was cheap and cheerful. Not dark and expensive like some of the uptown bistros that aped New York. I felt comfortable here, enveloped in the aroma of freshly brewed, rich coffee. Is there any better smell in the world?

"You need to get back on the horse," said Angela, pointing a perfectly manicured finger at me.

"Don't be a nag," I quipped, putting my mug down.

Angela was my best friend. I'd known her since high school. She and Zack had met each other three years ago. Now she was happily married and wanted everyone else to be. That's the sort of nice person she was. But she could also be kind of pushy.

"You have to tell me every detail," she ordered. "Of every date you go on."

"Of course I will!" I said. No I won't, I thought.

Angela is a great pal, but she works as a hair stylist. I know better than to tell her all the gory details. That hair salon thrives on gossip.

Of course, Angela always looks fabulous. Perfect hair, dyed a fashionable blond, with a great cut.

My hair is pretty ordinary, long and chocolate brown. I can't complain, because Angela gives me a great deal on cuts. And I like my natural hair color. It matches my eyes.

We are different in other ways too. Angela is outgoing. I'm more quiet. Angela is like glamorous Ginger on *Gilligan's Island*. I'm a Mary Ann.

"Let's call this Operation Prince Charming. I like that," she said, obviously pleased with herself. "Operation PC for short, in case anyone is listening in."

I grinned back at her. "Cute. Sort of like we're on a secret mission."